This book is dedicated to m Maegan, Noelan, and Madis followed the rules in school, I'm sure.

I also dedicate this book to all the children I taught in my kindergarten teaching career. They always kept me laughing with their funny antics and enthusiasm for school.

My name is Lillie- with an "e" at the end.

Tomorrow is my first day of kindergarten...

...and I am soooo excited!

...and make new friends.

I'm also excited to learn to read and write...

...and count to 100.

There is one teeny-tiny thing I am NOT excited about...

My friend Abdul is in second grade so he knows a lot about school.

He said there are LOTS of rules in school.

So **if** **I** were the teacher, **I** would make some changes.

If I were the teacher...

...there would be no rules in kindergarten.

If I were the teacher...

...you could sit wherever you wanted.

If I were the teacher...

...you could wear anything you wanted.

If I were the teacher...

...you could cut anything and everything.

If I were the teacher...

...you could use as much glue as you wanted.

If I were the teacher...

...you could make as much noise as you wanted.

...and do anything at recess.

Okay, maybe one or two rules would keep us safe and help us learn-and nobody will mind one tiny unicorn.

RULES

-Be safe

-Be kind

-Be helpful

-Do your best

-Only 1 tiny unicorn

29

Time for a Class Discussion

What rules do you think will help your class be safe and learn?

Talk with a friend and then share with an adult.

This page is designed to help adults facilitate a discussion with children about what rules are important.

Made in the USA
Las Vegas, NV
03 August 2023

75575890R00019